ZYXT
Joseph Clayton Mills
Second edition, 2012

WHAT IS A FRIEND? A SINGLE SOUL IN TWO BODIES

Aristotle

ADOLESCENCE

I have a friend who is afflicted with a remarkably acute and unusual variety of claustrophobia.

This curious anxiety first manifested itself in my friend's late adolescence, when, midway through the course of a particularly grueling and humiliating school day, he was suddenly overcome with the terrifying sensation of being tightly shut up within the narrow, suffocating confines of his own body. He became acutely aware of peering out from behind his eyes as if through the barred windows of a cell, and his panic-stricken heart thrashed against his ribs like the desperate wings of a caged bird.

From the day on which this sensation of claustrophobia first overwhelmed him, my friend has devoted much careful thought to devising a means by which he might escape from his unbearable prison alive. Sadly, he has met, as of yet, with very little success.

BARBER

I have a friend who has served as my barber for the past twenty years. My decades of patronage have been justified, as you might imagine, by the fact that my friend, although generally somewhat taciturn and possessed of a remarkably dour demeanor, has always performed his task with a preternatural skill. Indeed, it would not be too much to say that his haircuts have been uniformly characterized by a tastefulness bordering on the sublime, reflecting the meticulous care with which my friend labors over each snip and clip of the scissors and every supple caress of the straight razor. Rising from the polished chrome and patent leather throne of his barber chair, I would invariably discover nary a hair out of place, for—like all to whom I apply the sobriquet "Maestro"—my friend imposed upon himself standards of blinding, relentless perfection.

Several weeks ago, however, much to my surprise and dismay, I arrived for my two-thirty appointment to discover that my friend had been arrested for the murder and decapitation of three of his best and most loyal customers. He was discovered in the gleaming florescent confines of his barber shop, leafing calmly through a tattered, well-thumbed gentleman's magazine while the headless corpses of his victims each sat patiently in one of the shop's three hydraulic-lift barber chairs. Offering no struggle, my friend surrendered meekly to the authorities, by all accounts expressing nothing more than mild surprise at the seriousness with which the constabulary seemed to regard his altogether gruesome crime. Oddly, the heads of his victims have yet to be recovered.

Under interrogation, my friend has since attempted to justify his actions by insisting that he had meant no harm to his unfortunate victims, but had been motivated solely by an overwhelming compulsion, after a lifetime devoted to the barber's art, to resolve the so-called hair dilemma, as he phrased it, once and for all.

Unfortunately, despite my repeated assurances that I am willing to shoulder the perhaps considerable risk, the medical authorities entrusted with my former barber's care inform me that it would be quite out of the question to allow my friend to lay hands once again on the tools of his trade, and they have thus far remained unresponsive to my repeated and insistent requests that he be permitted to give me a quick trim during one of my not infrequent pilgrimages to the asylum where he remains confined.

It is difficult to see the pain that fills my friend's large and rather soulful eyes when, during these visits, he is confronted with my increasingly unkempt locks and lengthening, decidedly unruly beard. True, I might easily find another barber and thus ease my friend's discomfort. But where will I ever be assured of finding another capable of approaching the task with the same admirable, if unsettling, zeal?

COMPOSITION

I have a friend who was once a rather well-known composer. As a young man, he had achieved a good deal of renown upon the debut of his *Schopenhauer Requiem*, hailed as something of a minor masterpiece owing to its seamless blending of operatic and liturgical forms. Several years ago, however, my friend was witness to a rather horrific tragedy that served to bring an untimely end to his theretofore promising musical career.

While teaching a master class at the most prestigious musical academy in Salzburg, my friend's lecture on counterpoint was rudely interrupted when the electrical wiring—which, incidentally, was well over one hundred years old, having been installed in the waning days of the Hapsburg Empire—burst into flames. The venerable building that housed the musical academy was rapidly consumed by the ensuing conflagration. Fortunately, my friend was able to quickly make his escape by leaping, with a degree of athleticism heretofore unsuspected, from a second-story window to the ground below. Many of his unfortunate young pupils, alas, remained trapped inside the musical academy, beyond hope of rescue. In a state of shock, my friend was held completely transfixed by the spectacle. For some time, the terrified screams of the children filled the air, mingling with the roar of the flames, the impotent wailing of the fire department's sirens, and the curiously melodic snapping of piano strings as, one by one, the academy's priceless collection of Steinways was devoured.

Alongside the music that he had heard on that terrifyingly cloudless afternoon in Salzburg, he later confessed, his own earlier work—although it had been widely praised for its power, profundity, and spiritual insight—could henceforth only strike him as a wretchedly inadequate sham. Dismissing his previous efforts as hopelessly naive, he immediately threw himself into his work with renewed purpose and intensity.

However, despite his best efforts and his impressive reputation, my friend has thus far been unable to find an orchestra willing to add his new works to their repertoire. The reason for this neglect, I am afraid, is patently obvious. Since that fateful day in Salzburg, my friend's every composition has contained—alongside those parts scored for conventional instrumentation, such as woodwinds, strings, and brass—one to be sung by a choir of "Children in Great Torment." The situation is most unfortunate, not only for my friend but for all lovers of great music, for it is abundantly clear from even the most cursory examination of the score that, were these works ever to be performed, the result would prove to be exquisitely beautiful.

DOG

I had a friend who, to his never-ending irritation, was regarded by even his closest acquaintances as a horrible specimen of misanthropy. Of course, he regarded himself in quite a different light, insisting that the vocal attacks upon the hypocrisy, cruelty, and idiocy of his friends and neighbors which had earned him his reputation for misanthropy were motivated, on the contrary, by a deep and abiding love for humanity. In fact, it was precisely his idealistic vision of mankind's capacity for the noble and virtuous, he claimed, that made his daily confrontations with what he invariably characterized as "humanity's beastly propensity for the base and vile" so difficult to endure in silence.

One afternoon, however, as we partook of our weekly chess match at my favorite café, my friend confided to me—by way of explanation for his uncharacteristically clumsy attempt at the Sicilian defense—that he feared that his bitter despair over the sorry condition of his fellow man was beginning to take a toll upon his psychological well-being. In fact, he admitted that, in recent months, he had found himself struggling with a near-constant depression and, in addition, was overwhelmed beneath the crushing burden of loneliness. He informed me that, to his mild embarrassment, I was the only person who he could still consider as a friend, all others having been driven beyond endurance by his violent tirades.

Concerned, I advised my friend to consider acquiring a dog. A canine companion, I suggested, would surely help to alleviate his loneliness, and he might find that the creature's steadfast loyalty and cheerful disposition would encourage him to adopt a more positive attitude himself.

To my surprise, my friend seemed quite taken with the suggestion. He confessed to me that, in the days of his youth, he had desperately craved a puppy. Alas, his parents, finding the preservation of their expensive oriental rugs to take precedence over the happiness of their only child and heir, had always forbidden it. Nonetheless, to this day he preserved a certain fondness for the species.

Several weeks later, having endured a string of unexplained cancellations of our chess match, I chanced to encounter my friend in the park near his apartment. He was leading an enthusiastic Jack Russell terrier on a long leather leash. As I approached, my friend greeted me with a surprisingly cheerful smile and, admonishing his terrier to sit, launched into a profuse expression of gratitude. He had taken my advice to heart and had immediately acquired his dog at the local pound. I congratulated my now-ebullient friend upon his acquisition and must confess to feeling rather pleased that my offhanded advice had yielded such positive results so rapidly.

Over the course of the next several months, I often encountered my friend in that same park, always accompanied by his rambunctious terrier. Whenever we chanced to meet, my friend would proceeded to regale me with a seemingly endless stream of anecdotes concerning the peculiar talents of his dog, making special mention of his facility at retrieving a well-soiled tennis ball, his ready obedience to various commands, and his fierce loyalty. Indeed, my friend seemed incapable of conversing on any other topic. Whereas he had once been unable to hold a conversation that did not exude the darkest waves of pessimism concerning the state of humanity, he was now brimming with praise for the seemingly inexhaustible virtues of his dog. The metamorphosis that his pet had wrought in my friend was a wonder to behold. Indeed, this new companion seemed to eradicate the last vestigial traces of my friend's need for human contact, for I began to encounter him less and less often in what had once been his usual haunts. No longer could I count on finding him sipping espresso in the local coffee shop or browsing in the dark confines of his favorite antiquarian bookseller.

Later that winter, however, I once again chanced upon my friend in the park. The leafless trees stood black against the snow that lightly robed the frozen ground. My friend huddled, bundled from his head to his toe, with a long scarf wound tightly about his neck and a black wool cap pulled down about his red-rimmed ears, on an ice-encrusted park bench. Surprisingly, his diminutive terrier was nowhere to be seen.

I greeted my friend warmly, and in return I received no more than a curt nod of recognition. Undeterred, I took a seat alongside my friend and attempted to engage him in conversation. Soon, his terse monosyllables had given way to a passionate diatribe against the sickening incompetence of his colleagues at the university, and he singled out one well-respected Shakespearean scholar as only the most particularly egregious example of a moral depravity and intellectual shoddiness that pervaded the academy.

Somewhat taken aback by my friend's violent reversion to his misanthropic ways, I cautiously broached the subject of his missing dog. I hoped, I said, that nothing had befallen him.

"I poisoned the beast," my friend replied.

Astounded, I could only wait patiently for my friend to explain.

"Only last week," he said, his breath forming pale clouds in the cold air, "I was perfectly content. In fact, I was sitting by the hearth of my roaring fireplace reading Voltaire with the fellow nestled snugly in my lap. I believe that I was lightly scratching him behind the left ear, which was a ritual we both enjoyed tremendously. As I reflected upon the remarkable happiness that this little dog had so unexpectedly brought into my life, it occurred to me, quite suddenly, that if I were to admit the truth to myself, it was clear I loved this little dog more than any creature I had ever known. Neither filial devotion nor conjugal bliss could compare with this one simple moment by the roaring fire. But more than this—to my intense shame, I was overcome with the realization that I loved him with a love that dwarfed the love that I felt for Humanity itself. If at that moment I had been given the choice between saving the life of Mahatma Gandhi from the assassin's bullet, on the one hand, and saving the life of my little dog, on the other, I would have chosen that of my scruffy terrier without a second thought. With a certain horror, I realized that, in fact, I would rather bear witness to the slaughter of nameless millions than to endure the sight of my dog suffering a single scratch."

I was silent. My friend turned his face toward me, and I could see that his expression was one of desolation.

"I immediately hurried to the store and purchased a sizable quantity of rat poison. What else, in good conscience, could I possibly have done?"

ENNUI

I had a friend who, having hurled himself from a great height, was annoyed to discover that, in marked contrast to what he had been lead to expect, the brief moments in which the ground hurtled up with ever greater clarity to greet him were marked by neither a heightened intensity of sensorial experience nor by a mystical epiphany of the preciousness of life. Rather, the rapid seconds of his fall were quite as suffused with boredom and ennui—and passed just as slowly—as every other moment in his short, yet interminable, existence.

FOOLPROOF

I have a friend who has developed a foolproof method for forming his opinion on any given topic. Seated across from me at a recent dinner party, he admitted to me that he simply chooses someone whom he despises, elicits their views on a subject —for example, the current state of the American novel, the wisdom of a flat tax, or the impact of the Dreyfus affair on French social thought—and then proceeds to construct his own opinions along precisely the opposite lines. In this way, he assured me, he was guaranteed an accurate barometer in all matters of taste, morality, and public conduct.

When I congratulated him on the brilliance of his method, however, he appeared aghast. He immediately became depressed and, despite my efforts to draw him into conversation, maintained a sullen silence for the remainder of the evening.

GRADUATE SCHOOL

On the verge of earning a PhD in economics from one of the more prestigious of the second-tier universities, having assiduously devoted himself entirely to academic study for a dozen years to the exclusion of all else, and indeed having sacrificed any semblance of a so-called personal life for the sake of his scholarly pursuits, a close friend of mine was struck a severe blow when his mentor—to whose groundbreaking theories my friend had long been a fanatical adherent and to the defense of whom all of my friend's own work was slavishly devoted—committed suicide at the age of eighty-three by placing his head in an oven.

Compounding my friend's misfortune, his beloved mentor had left for posterity a lengthy suicide note in which he completely repudiated all of his former work, demonstrating with the aid of recent insights derived from game theory that the ostensibly groundbreaking work to which he owed his considerable fame in academic circles was completely nonsensical.

Several weeks later, crushed by the twin disasters of his mentor's self-asphyxiation and the utter discrediting of those theories that had formed the foundation upon which the entire edifice of his nearly completed dissertation was constructed, my friend surprised no one when he chose to follow once again in his mentor's footsteps, although electing to carry out his own suicide by means of hanging, rather than by placing his head in an oven.

His own suicide note, however—forty-seven densely footnoted pages, discovered lying in a neat stack on the battered crate that had served his wretched studio apartment as both a makeshift office and a kitchen table—gave his fellow graduate students, myself included, something of a shock, for it proved to consist entirely of a vicious, scathing, and altogether brilliant critique of what my late friend repeatedly referred to as his mentor's "suicide methodology." Displaying to the fullest those formidable analytic skills that had promised him a glorious future in the academy, my friend devoted himself to savaging his mentor's predilection for death by asphyxiation, while vigorously espousing, with especial reference to Melville's *Billy Budd*, Judas Iscariot, and French aesthete Gérard de Nerval, the manifold virtues of death by hanging.

I must confess that my mood brightened somewhat with the knowledge that, in this final gesture, my friend had managed—briefly, but decisively—to step out from under his master's shadow.

HUMOR

I have a friend whom I long suspected was completely lacking in a sense of humor. For almost a decade, the two of us had worked in the same cramped insurance office, literally toiling side by side, and in all the years of our acquaintance I had never seen him so much as crack a smile at even the most uproarious water-cooler witticism. In addition, I had noticed his frequent confusion whenever, in the course of our conversations, I attempted to employ a so-called ironic tone. As you might imagine, his deadly serious demeanor limited our personal relations to the most stolid and matter-of-fact interactions.

When, much against my wishes, I was compelled to accompany my friend on a business trip to a distant city, I was surprised to discover that my earlier conclusions about his sense of humor—or, rather, lack thereof—were quite mistaken.

On arrival at our hotel, he immediately began to peruse the residential pages of the local telephone book. When I inquired as to whose number he was searching for, he admitted, with some small embarrassment, that whenever he found himself in a new city he felt compelled to examine the telephone book for listings under the name "Hitler." It was, he explained, an understandably uncommon but not yet entirely extinct surname.

Having discovered a single listing, for one "Edith Hitler" of 4444 North Magnolia Avenue, and with nothing else to do in preparation for the presentation we would be called upon to provide our client the following morning, my friend and I whiled away the remainder of the evening placing a series of admittedly juvenile but nonetheless rather amusing prank telephone calls to Mrs. Hitler. With the aid of several bourbons, courtesy of the minibar, we were soon reduced to paroxysms of laughter.

My friend proved to possess a laugh that, under most circumstances, would be described as hearty and good natured, if a trifle high in pitch. However, I must admit that the unfamiliar sight of my friend's laughing face—contorted beyond recognition, wheezing and red, with its teeth bared in a maniacal grin—struck me for some reason as an extraordinarily unnerving spectacle.

INSULT

I once had a friend who, over the long course of many years, gradually began to take on, as if by a process of osmosis, all of those quirks, opinions, and traits of character that I had always considered to be most deeply my own.

When I first made his acquaintance, for example, my friend had shown a marked preference for the sentimental excesses of the films of Hollywood's so-called Golden Age over the headier intellectual pleasures that characterized Italian neorealist cinema. After several years, however, he began to espouse, with equal fervor, precisely the opposite opinion; that is, a preference for Antonioni and Visconti over Capra, Hawks, and Sturges—an opinion that I had myself defended in his presence on occasions too numerous to mention.

Indeed, it would not be exaggerating the point to say that my friend's entire worldview incrementally conformed itself to my own. He was initially a devout Hegelian, and this despite my constant entreaties that he lend more credence to Nietzsche's critique of the dialectic; after several years I was amazed to discover that, completely without my knowledge and, as it were, on the sly, he had entirely thrown over Hegel for Nietzsche.

Nor was my friend immune to aping even the most superficial aspects of my character. When I first made his acquaintance, he was an inveterate smoker of Gauloise cigarettes; in time, he came to develop an insatiable addiction to my own beloved Cuban cigars. Once indifferent to sporting contests, he learned to emulate my fascination with amateur boxing. Formerly scrupulously clean-shaven, he eventually went so far as to attempt to cultivate my distinctive handlebar mustache.

Initially, I found his tendency to adopt even my most eccentric mannerisms and opinions flattering—even charming—and I frequently congratulated myself on having exerted such a salutary effect on my young protégé's development. Over time, however, as his mimicry grew ever more exact, I became increasingly disturbed. To my surprise, I found that the more perfectly my friend came to resemble me, the less pleasure I took in his company, until at last, as his performance was polished to a mirror like exactitude, I found it quite impossible to be in his presence for even the slightest length of time. I avoided him as assiduously as I could, although the similarities in our habits and predilections led to inevitable run-ins at the tobacconist, the gymnasium, and the barber. On each occasion, somewhat to my consternation, I was consumed by a virulent loathing that I could only conceal with the greatest exertion of personal will.

Fortunately, my friend's abrupt and unexpected suicide alleviated the need for further social contact. Leaving a note that characterized his life as "a ludicrous farce no longer worth the trouble of living," he had ingested a generous handful of prescription painkillers before hurling himself from the balcony of his tony downtown apartment.

I must confess that my immediate and somewhat embarrassing relief at his untimely demise was tempered by the troubling question of whether that life which he had so abruptly discarded and to which his suicide note had referred with such derision should truly be regarded as his own—and his final act merely the ultimate step in a process of self-annihilation that had perhaps begun with our first acquaintance—or whether, on the contrary, his suicide should be taken as the most outrageous insult to which I have ever been subjected.

JUSTICE

I have a friend who was recently arrested for the murder of his young wife, the beautiful and charming heiress to a large munitions fortune.

The young couple, married for less than a year, had been sharing a romantic evening alone together aboard the smaller of their two yachts when tragedy struck—according to my friend's initial account, in the form of a sudden mishap involving the mizzen mast. His wife, he declared, had been sent tumbling overboard into the curiously placid waters of Lake Michigan and, despite his valiant attempt to come to her rescue, had disappeared beneath the waves without further ado.

Suspicion, however, soon fell upon my unfortunate friend—particularly when it was discovered that the enormous sum which he stood to inherit had been supplemented with a recently acquired and inordinately large life insurance policy—and an arrest soon followed.

Of course, the body of the deceased was not forthcoming; as a result, the prosecution's case was of necessity constructed entirely from a mosaic of circumstantial—although admittedly compelling—evidence, hinging largely on my friend's predilection for lavish spending, certain outstanding gambling debts, and the financial windfall that accompanied his wife's death. My friend's lawyers—not coincidentally, the best that money could buy—proceeded to mount a ferocious defense, painting my friend in the most favorable manner and inviting a string of witnesses to testify to the depth and profundity of the love that he had felt for his late wife, who was portrayed in an altogether saintly light. As the trial neared its end, it was widely assumed by those who had followed the proceedings most closely that, barring any mishaps, my friend was assured of an easy and early acquittal.

It therefore came as a complete shock to all concerned when, in the midst of closing arguments, my friend—who had listened to the prosecution's summation of their case with noticeable and ever-increasing agitation—rose from his chair and declared that he wished to change his plea from "not guilty" to "guilty." In the interest of justice, he announced, he would accept full culpability for his wife's death, with but a single condition—that it be publicly acknowledged that he had not murdered her in order to lay hands upon her sizeable fortune, as the prosecution claimed. The motivation for his wife's murder, my friend insisted, should be attributed solely to what he termed her "completely insufferable personality."

KINDNESS

I have a friend who is notorious in our circle for his remarkable lack of sympathy toward the plight of his fellow human beings. Despite being endowed with a sizable fortune, he makes it his practice to contribute not a shilling to even the most worthy of charitable causes. Moreover, his personal interactions are characterized by a vicious, callous disregard for the feelings of others that has often reduced his interlocutors to tears and is rumored to have driven at least one unfortunate soul, a professor of classical languages and amateur ornithologist, to suicide.

When I once inquired of my friend why he had adopted such an adversarial stance towards the world, he declared that he was quite as full of the milk of human kindness as anyone and, in fact, was altogether convinced that he possessed that particular commodity in far greater abundance than did the vast majority of the population.

"I realized long ago that compassion, kindness, and sympathy were in remarkably short supply in this world," he explained, "and since that time, I have been careful to hoard my allotted portion."

LOGIC

I have a friend who recently confided in me that, despite his wife's many avowals as to her absolute fidelity, he was nonetheless deeply concerned over the paternity of his young daughter and was haunted by the suspicion that the cherubic, pigtailed child he had so often bounced upon his knee was not, in fact, his daughter at all, but was, rather, the product of an illicit liaison with a so-called friend of the family.

It was clear to me from the desperate tone in his voice that my friend's quite possibly misguided suspicions were rapidly evolving into a potentially dangerous obsession. I was nonetheless quite shocked when my friend went on to confess that, earlier that same afternoon, he had strangled with his own hands both his young daughter and a coworker who was, at best, only a passing acquaintance.

When I inquired as to how my friend, in all respects a paragon of ethical, rational behavior, could bring himself to commit a pair of such horrific, irrational crimes, he hastened to explain that he possessed no animosity toward his admittedly innocent daughter, nor, for that matter, toward his unfortunate coworker. Rather, he explained, his express purpose had been to obtain, as he phrased it, an "irrefutable, logical proof" that would at last resolve the issue of his daughter's paternity with some finality. He reasoned that, insofar as the murder of one's daughter clearly constituted a decidedly more heinous crime than what he termed a "murder plain and simple," the sense of guilt and self-loathing that accompanied the young child's murder, if she were in truth his daughter, would greatly exceed that felt at the commission of the second crime.

Of course, I recommended to my friend that he hasten to submit himself to the authorities at once and, with his agreement, placed the necessary telephone calls. As we awaited the arrival of the patrol car that would take my friend into custody, however, I was unable to resist the temptation to inquire as to the outcome of his experiment.

My friend was able to report, with an expression conveying relief and despair in equal measure, that he had observed no discernable difference in the two sensations.

MUTUAL INTEREST

I once had a friend with whom I found myself in complete agreement on every imaginable subject.

Over the course of our acquaintanceship, we discovered that our taste in music, literature, and the arts was remarkably similar, involving a shared adoration of Bizet's *Carmen*, Cervantes' *Don Quixote*, and Michelangelo's *Pietà*. Moreover, our political opinions, when we finally dared to broach the subject, were striking in their similarity, even to the point of our mutual fascination with the utopian theories of Fourier and our vaguely Bonapartist leanings. Our views on metaphysics were equally compatible, and in both cases derived from an intense study of Spinoza's *Ethics*.

Oddly, the one point on which our agreement proved to be most profound and the last point of congruence that we discovered before our friendship suddenly, if not unexpectedly, dissolved, was the virulent and mutual distaste with which we regarded one another.

NIGHTINGALE

I have a friend who, as a lifelong devotee of Bizet, harbors great hopes that his young daughter might one day make a grand success upon the operatic stage.

Although she is still a mere toddler and is thus far incapable of forming with any facility even the simplest words in English (to say nothing of Italian), my friend insists that, even from the moment of her first postnatal cry, he has been able to detect in her voice the sure traces of a divine instrument.

In order to encourage in his daughter a proper love for all things sonorous, my friend installed in her bedroom a beautiful nightingale in a gilded cage. Its melodic trills, he hoped, would serve as a suitable influence upon his daughter's as yet inchoate musicality.

When, some days later, my friend discovered that his young daughter had smothered the nightingale with a silken pillow, he was, much to my surprise, neither horrified nor discouraged. On the contrary, he was transported with delight, and his face beamed as he related the story.

"After all, is not the foremost ingredient in the soul of any artist," he asked rhetorically and with an expression of perhaps justifiable pride, "an insatiable lust for the blood of one's rival?"

OEDIPUS

I have a friend who has achieved an extraordinary degree of international notoriety on two accounts: first, as an actor—he is widely held to be one of the finest thespians of his generation—and second, as the perpetrator of one of the more horrific and celebrated crimes in recent memory, one made all the more notorious on account of the substantial fame he had already acquired on the stage.

Compounding public interest in the affair has been the nature of the crime itself. One afternoon, my friend—in an apparent fit of insanity and prompted by no easily discernable motive—murdered his elderly father with a blow from a golf club. When his mother attempted to intervene, he turned upon her as well and had soon supplemented his initial crime of patricide with the even more perfidious acts of rape and incest. Several moments later, however, he apparently regained some small measure of lucidity and, overcome with horror at the sight of his crimes, proceeded to put out both of his eyes with one of his mother's hatpins before being quietly taken into custody by the authorities.

One hardly needs to point out the uncanny and surely coincidental resemblance of the circumstances of this crime to the plot of that most famous of the tragedies of Sophocles, *Oedipus Rex*. Even more remarkable, however—at least to my mind—is the fact that, in all of his years upon the stage, my friend had never played the role of Oedipus, nor had he ever shown a particular talent for or inclination toward tragic drama. His specialty, on the contrary, was that theatrical genre generally known as "musical comedy."

PRESENT

I have a friend who is nearing his eightieth birthday, in honor of which occasion an elaborate surprise party has been planned. As my friend is a noted political figure and public intellectual, the surprise party promises to number among its guests an array of celebrities and dignitaries, including prominent politicians, a film actress of some renown, and a Nobel Prize-winning physicist. Understandably, I have been eagerly awaiting the occasion for some weeks now.

Recently, however, I have been troubled by the difficulty of selecting an appropriate birthday present for my friend, a man upon whom life has already bestowed so many gifts. For more than fifty years, he has led what might be described as a charmed career in public service. He has been rewarded with the accolades of his countrymen, great wealth, and a full and rich family life. His first wife, the daughter of an oil tycoon and noted philanthropist, provided him with a sizable fortune, several children, and thirty years of steadfast devotion before her sudden and almost painless death from a stroke. Having retained both his rugged good looks and his personal charm well into his old age, my friend was lucky enough to marry again, this time to a strikingly beautiful ballerina forty years his junior. Since retiring from public life, he has turned his hand to literature, penning several novels that have been quite well received, both critically and commercially. Indeed, as his eightieth year approaches he seems to have gathered into his possession all that life has to offer.

As the date of the surprise party grows nearer, I have been plagued by the question of what might constitute an appropriate gift for such a man. I have wandered from shop to shop, handling a kaleidoscopic array of curios, etchings, silk scarves, and fine Mont Blanc pens, each bauble more unsuitable than the last.

While despondently perusing rare first editions in the shop of an antiquarian book dealer of my acquaintance, however, the perfect gift at last occurred to me. Unfortunately, that gift is one beyond my power to bestow: a guidebook to the realm of the dead.

QUARTERFINALS

I once had a friend who, having triumphed over the brightest lights of our fifth grade class by correctly navigating the etymological minefield of "insouciant," was selected to represent our school in the state spelling bee championship.

I well remember the intensity with which he prepared for the looming competition. For several long weeks, he was not to be seen without an Oxford English Dictionary (unabridged) in tow. His every free moment was devoted to pouring, furrow-browed, over its entries as if bending the entire force of his eager young will to the Herculean task of memorizing the English language from "aardvark" to "zyxt." It was clear to even the casual observer that he was awash in dreams of glory and aspired to advance even unto the National finals.

Nevertheless, despite his extraordinary efforts and his indisputable talents, when the day of the competition finally arrived my friend was eliminated in the very first round of the quarter finals after failing to account for the second "t" in spelling the not especially difficult word "regrettably."

This unfortunate mishap was forcefully recalled to my mind more than fifty years later when, in reading my friend's admittedly hastily scribbled suicide note, I happened to notice that he had misspelled the word "regrettably" once again. The answer to the question of whether the inclusion of this particular misspelling in my friend's suicide note was merely an unlucky and somewhat pathetic coincidence or, on the contrary, a deliberate indication of his steadfast refusal to compromise with a world that, when all is said and done, had indeed treated him rather cruelly, is one that regrettably died with him.

ROUTINE OPERATION

I have a friend who, in the course of a long and illustrious career as one of the world's foremost neurosurgeons, has acquired but a single blemish upon an otherwise sterling professional reputation.

Once, in the midst of an extremely delicate operation, during the course of which the life of the patient—a television mogul who had once been a ballroom dancing champion of some renown—hung by a thread, my friend was seized by a fit of spontaneous, uncontrollable laughter that made proceeding with the operation quite impossible.

Despite a concerted attempt to regain his composure, my friend found that his hysteria only grew more difficult to control as the gravity of the patient's already quite precarious situation increased. The frantic admonitions of the anesthesiologist to the effect that, unless my friend composed himself immediately, the patient would surely expire upon the table only served to compound the difficulty, driving his mirth to new and seemingly insurmountable heights. Convulsed with laughter, my friend was finally forced to flee the operating theater altogether. This unexpected turn of events, needless to say, produced the direst of consequences for his unfortunate patient.

My friend assures me, however, that this curious incident, now some years in the past, was a complete—and, to him, quite inexplicable—aberration and should in no way impinge upon my confidence in his abilities or cause me in any way to question my decision to entrust myself to his hands during my upcoming surgery, which, my friend maintains, promises to be in all respects a routine operation.

SÉANCE

I had a friend who was thrown into a deep despondency in the wake of the accidental deaths of his wife and young son.

Nonetheless, it was with some surprise that I recently received an invitation from my friend—formerly a hardened skeptic—to join him in attending a séance convened for the express purpose of placing him once again in contact with his departed loved ones. To my dismay, he had seemingly fallen in thrall to a Ouija board-wielding charlatan—to be precise, an ancient, one-eyed crone of Romanian extraction—in whose powers he placed the utmost confidence and upon whom he seemed willing to squander his entire fortune in the slim hope that she might somehow be able to effect a reunion of his sundered family. The séance, my friend informed me, was to be held in the cramped confines of his family sepulcher on the following Sunday—a date that happened to coincide with the first anniversary of the unfortunate deaths of his wife and child. It would be a great honor, he said, if I would be kind enough to lend my participation to this event. Curious to observe at first hand the results of my friend's supernatural obsession—and, if possible, save him from the clutches of this turbaned swindler—I readily accepted his invitation.

At the last possible moment, however, I was unavoidably detained by a recurrence of that severe and debilitating depression that has plagued me all my life, which made rising from the comforting confines of my four-poster bed quite impossible. Never, however, have I been more thankful for my melancholic disposition. In this instance, at least, I owe it my life—for when I opened the next morning's newspaper, it was only to discover, to my horror, that an unspeakable tragedy had befallen my grieving friend and his companions.

According to the published account, the mausoleum's poor ventilation, when combined with an inordinate profusion of candles, incense, and burning censers, had resulted in the deaths by asphyxiation, en masse, of all those participating in the séance.

I took what solace I could from the fact that the unfortunate victims seemed not to have suffered overmuch. It was readily apparent that they were quite unaware of their impending fate, as testified to by the fact that their corpses were discovered seated peacefully in a circle about the medium's table, hands clasped and eyes closed in profound meditation. To all appearances, in fact, it seemed as if they were still deeply engaged in their ill-fated attempt to contact that world from which no traveler returns—an attempt that, despite my skeptical nature, I am willing to concede proved to be an indisputable success.

TELESCOPE

I had a friend who was a well-known astronomer, having made his considerable reputation through the discovery, after long years of silent contemplation of the heavens with the aid of a special deep space radio telescope of his own invention, of several previously undiscovered celestial bodies.

When reading of his latest exploits in the journals of astronomical science, I always marveled to reflect on how far he had come since those half-forgotten days when, as mere boys, we had together conducted our earliest tentative backyard experiments with the cheap telescope that I had received for my eleventh birthday, and I recalled with affection the many happy hours that we had spent together spying the rings of Saturn or tracing the curious meandering of some wayward, arcing comet.

While going through my friend's scattered papers and notes after his recent suicide, I came across one particular entry in his diary—kept with remarkable diligence over many years—that has inexplicably continued to haunt me.

In it, he confided that he could not shake the melancholy suspicion that the words and gestures and sentiments of even those individuals whom he considered to be closest to him had been transmitted across a distance too vast to contemplate, traveling to reach him through great, unimaginable voids and that—like those faint stars to the study of which he had devoted his entire life, whose light is but the lingering trace of long-dead suns— the source of these beautiful visions, too, had long since burned away.

UNREMARKABLE

I have a friend who is, in all respects, rather unremarkable.

In appearance he is nondescript, of average height, and with regular features—a medium-sized nose, an undistinguished mouth, two eyes that, in all likelihood, are brown—although I confess that I've never quite noticed their color, and, if pressed, would concede that they might very well be hazel. As for eccentric mannerisms, he has none. I know him to possess no especial talents, nor any particular interests, habits, or passions. I can recall no interesting anecdotes of which he is the subject.

In fact, I find it impossible to explain why I'm discussing him at all.

VOICE

I have a friend who was once a deeply religious man, but whose faith has recently suffered a setback.

A fully ordained priest, he several months ago shocked his congregation by resigning from the clergy and turning immediately to copious amounts of drink. The reason for this seeming crisis of faith remained shrouded in mystery.

Concerned by the sudden upheaval in my friend's life, I paid him a visit in the studio apartment that he had recently rented in a nearby "singles complex." The place was a complete shambles. Empty bottles of off-brand bourbon littered the small, dingy room, and it was clear from the profusion of Chinese takeout boxes scattered about that my friend had been spending the majority of his time slumped in a drunken stupor in front of the perpetually flickering television set.

I had feared that my friend would be reluctant to discuss the curious change that had come over him, but once the subject was broached, he poured forth his sad story with abandon. After many years of devout prayer, he explained, he had at last been granted a privilege and honor reserved for only the most faithful and fervent of believers. Several months ago, lost in meditation and fasting, he had heard the voice of God.

Oddly, however, this almost unprecedented confirmation of the existence of the divinity had served not to amplify his faith but, on the contrary, to erode it completely.

When I inquired, astounded, as to how this could possibly be, my friend flushed red with embarrassment. When the voice of God had spoken to him, he explained, it had been marred, much to his horror and surprise, by a decidedly effeminate lisp.

WILL

I had a friend who stipulated in his last will and testament, the reading of which I recently had the melancholy honor of attending, that half of his vast fortune—the product of many years of canny real estate speculation—be donated to the medical research university where he endured his final days. The will indicated that these funds were to be used for the express purpose of establishing a center for advanced research on cancer of the prostate, that disease which, in his own words, had left his body "a horrific ruin."

The validity of my friend's will, however, has since been successfully challenged by his understandably irate children, on the grounds that their father was clearly not, despite his claims to the contrary, of sound mind during its drafting. The most damning piece of evidence to be offered at the hearing, paradoxically, was the will itself. In addition to designating that fifty percent of my friend's fortune be set aside for prostate cancer research, the will stipulated that the entirety of the remaining portion be donated to the Catholic Church for the express purpose of establishing an advanced research center devoted to the study of the third of the seven deadly sins, that of Avarice, which, my friend's will maintained—again in his own words—had left his soul "mutilated beyond all recognition."

X

I had a friend who, in the aftermath of an acrimonious break-up with a former lover, insisted that the young lady in question return to him all of the items that he had given her over the course of the affair, including—but not limited to—an expensive mink stole, a first edition of Rilke's *Sonnets to Orpheus*, and an extraordinarily ostentatious diamond engagement ring (this last bestowed upon the lovely but fickle object of his affection several months prior to the dissolution of their ill-fated romance). To all of these demands, his former lover readily acquiesced.

However, when my friend further insisted upon retrieving his idealism, his youth, and his confidence in a future suffused with possibility, all of which he claimed to have entrusted to her keeping, she simply laughed, less at the absurdity of his request than at the absolute, desperate sincerity with which it was made.

YOUNG MAN

I have a friend who is a successful state's attorney. He has recently begun to receive a great deal of public notoriety, having served as chief prosecutor in several of our city's more sensational murder trials, and his name is no longer an uncommon sight in the daily papers.

Soon after making his acquaintance, I attended a cocktail party at my new friend's spacious suburban home. During the course of the evening, I happened to note that, on the wall of his well-appointed study, there hung the photograph of a smiling young man in a cap and gown. I took the photograph to be that of the chief prosecutor's eldest son, whom I knew had recently matriculated at my own alma mater. Congratulating my friend on having such a handsome son, I remarked that the resemblance between them—for they shared the same aquiline nose, the same wan smile, and something penetrating if somewhat remote that lingered in their gray eyes—was quite extraordinary.

My friend quickly corrected my mistake. The young man whose photograph hung on the wall of his study was not his son, he explained. Rather, the photograph was of the first defendant whom my friend had had the pleasure, as he put it, of sending to the electric chair. Any seeming familial resemblance, he insisted, was purely coincidental.

ZEBRA CROSSING

I had a friend who had been, since earliest childhood, a fanatical Anglophile. His intense devotion to his invalid mother had, alas, long prevented him from ever visiting the land that had so captured his imagination; however, immediately upon his mother's not-unexpected demise, he began to plan the journey that he had dreamed of for so many years and which, on more than one occasion, I had heard him refer to as the fulfillment of a lifelong ambition. In truth, despite his recent bereavement, I had never seen him quite as suffused with joy as he was on the day that I saw him off on his journey. Bidding me a fond farewell, he promised to dispatch me a postcard at the earliest opportunity to apprise me of his adventures.

By an eerie coincidence, however, the postcard in question arrived some days after I was informed by transatlantic cable that my friend, having inadvertently glanced in the wrong direction while crossing the street, had been struck and killed by one of the city's notorious double-decker buses.

Obviously, the postcard had simply been dropped into a mailbox prior to my friend's unexpected demise, and its belated arrival was surely attributable to nothing more mysterious than the vicissitudes of the transatlantic post; nonetheless, for me this final missive took on an inescapably eerie resonance. In the weeks that followed, I found myself returning to it again and again, reading and rereading the terse message scribbled on the back in handwriting as familiar and intimate as the sound of my unfortunate friend's now-silenced voice: "The weather is lovely. Having a wonderful time. Wish you were here."

Close scrutiny revealed a host of small coincidences and inconsistencies—the inadequate postage which had nonetheless somehow sufficed to bring the postcard to my doorstep, the curiously illegible postmark, and, not least, the glossy full-color photograph of a red double-decker bus that graced its obverse side—the sum total of which, to my perhaps feverish imagination, eventually came to seem incontrovertible proofs that this message had indeed originated, not in the so-called United Kingdom but, rather, in a far more inaccessible, mysterious, and exotic land—that undiscovered country which lies beyond the grave.

To this day, I cannot help approaching my mailbox with an overwhelming, uncanny sense of mingled anticipation and dread, despite the fact that no further communiqué has thus far been forthcoming.

www.ingramcontent.com/pod-product-compliance
Ingram Content Group UK Ltd.
Pitfield, Milton Keynes, MK11 3LW, UK
UKHW020227250726
13967UKWH00001B/240